The Linney Twins
Get Cooking

by Natalie Lewis
illustrated by Mike Cressy

 HOUGHTON MIFFLIN   BOSTON

Printed in China

ISBN-13: 978-0-547-02227-7
ISBN-10: 0-547-02227-1

8 9 10 0940 15 14 13
4500396701

Liv Linney opens her eyes to another lazy summer day. She doesn't even have to look at the clock to find out the time.

"The hour is ten o'clock in the morning," a voice announces from the hallway.

It is the year 2157. Liv's world relies almost completely on computers that control machines and tools.

A voice comes from the hallway.

In the next room, Liv's twin brother, Luke Linney, climbs out of bed, rubbing his eyes and yawning. Seconds later, the bed is already made.

"Thanks," Luke says. "Hey. How many days until school starts?"

"School starts in forty-seven days," the voice continues. "Today is July 17th. The year is 2157."

"Great, plenty of time to do nothing," Luke responds.

Liv and Luke's home is never dirty.

The average child in Luke and Liv's fourth-grade class never has to do any chores. Sure, they could *choose* to take out the trash or make their own beds. But why do something themselves when someone or something else can do everything for them?

For Liv and Luke, that something is Derek.

Derek is a robot. He doesn't just make beds. He vacuums, does laundry, and even washes windows.

Liv and Luke got Derek when they were in the second grade, and the three of them are great friends. Luke even lets Derek play with the family dog, Lucy.

Derek even plays with Lucy, the family dog.

After breakfast, Liv and Luke plop onto their favorite places on the sofa. They check different stations on the family television, but they don't waste an ounce of energy because their robot also operates the remote control.

"Turn to the music station, Derek," Luke orders the robot.

"I want to watch baseball," Liv says.

This makes things difficult because a robot can't obey one owner more than another.

Still, Liv somehow wins their dispute. Baseball it is.

Three hours later, Liv and Luke are still glued to the set.

"Hey guys," their mother asks. "Why don't you turn off the TV and do something fun?"

"This *is* fun," the twins respond.

"I get that. But don't you want to do something different for a change?"

Life in 2157 is not as exciting as you might think!

"I know what I want to do," Luke announces. "Derek, what's for lunch?"

There is no response.

"Derek?" Luke calls, his eyes still glued to the television.

After a few seconds, he turns to look at the robot. It is frozen in place. Nothing Luke says or does can make him move.

Derek has stopped moving.

The robot repairman arrives an hour later.

"Nothing I can do right now ma'am," he announces to the twins' mother after inspecting the robot. He tells the family that they need a special part, which will take a couple of days to arrive.

"I want a second opinion," Liv demands.

"I can get our head inspector over here. But she'll probably tell you the same thing," the repairman replies.

"No, we'll be fine without Derek for a couple of days," Mrs. Linney responds.

"I guess we'll have to fix our own lunch," Mrs. Linney says.

Liv and Luke are frozen with shock.

Mrs. Linney grabs a big, old book. It looks like it hasn't been opened for centuries.

"This should be helpful," she says.

"What is it?" Liv asks.

"A cookbook. It belonged to my grandmother," Mrs. Linney explains.

"You mean *people* used to cook?" Luke asks.

Cooking is a new idea for the twins.

Cooking is fun.

After reading through the book, they decide to make lasagna. Mrs. Linney orders the ingredients from a market that delivers groceries to their door.

As soon as the food arrives, Mrs. Linney starts giving orders.

"Okay Luke," she says. "You grate some cheese while I slice these onions. Liv, you can boil the water for the pasta."

"Luke, get the meat while I put the pasta in this dish," Liv orders. "One layer of meat is placed over the pasta. Cheese is sprinkled over the meat. Repeat," they all read from the big book. "Bake lasagna for one-and-a-half hours."

"One-and-a-half *hours*?!" the twins shout. They can't believe they will have to wait so long to taste their creation.

Liv and Luke put the lasagna into the oven.

Lucy enjoys the extra attention.

"What are we going to do while we wait?"
Liv whines.

"Why don't you go outside and play?"
their mother suggests.

Liv and Luke look at each other curiously.
Suddenly, they do have more energy. They
dash outside to play with Lucy.

The twins have so much fun that they
actually lose track of time.

When they return to the kitchen more than two hours later, the lasagna is cooling on top of the metal countertop. It looks delicious.

"I can't believe we made this. What do you think of that?" replies Luke.

"I think, once he's fixed, we should give Derek a break, don't you?" smiles Liv.

"Yeah," Luke agrees. "We should cook more often."

"Now that you can cook, you can learn to make your beds, too!" their mother says.

Luke and Liv look at each other, giggling. "Maybe," they reply together. "Maybe not."

Responding

✔ **TARGET SKILL** **Author's Purpose** What was the author's purpose for writing this book? What details support this purpose? Copy and complete the chart below.

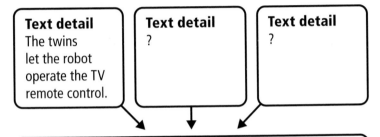

Text detail
The twins let the robot operate the TV remote control.

Text detail
?

Text detail
?

Purpose To show readers that using robots too much can make people lazy.

Write About It

Text to World Imagine that you have to write a research paper on different uses for robots. Brainstorm topics to include and then organize them into correct outline form.

15

average	inspector
calculated	mechanical
centuries	progress
dispute	superior
insert	waste

✔ **TARGET SKILL** **Author's Purpose** Use text details to figure out the author's reasons for writing.

✔ **TARGET STRATEGY** **Question** Ask questions before you read, as you read, and after you read.

GENRE Science Fiction is a fantasy story whose plot often depends on scientific ideas.